Gemma O'Neill Farrell was born and raised in Dublin, Ireland. She is married and has four children. Gemma has always had a love for children's books since having her first child, and the Uglybug is an idea she has wanted to put on paper for a long time in the hopes that the message of kindness will resonate with children and influence their impressionable minds.

THE MOST BEAUTIFUL UGLYBUG

GEMMA O'NEILL FARRELL

AUSTIN MACAULEY PUBLISHERS™

LONDON • CAMBRIDGE • NEW YORK • SHARJAH

A CIP catalogue record for this title is available from the British Library.

ISBN 9781398472990 (Paperback)
ISBN 9781398473003 (ePub e-book)

www.austinmacauley.com

First Published 2023
Austin Macauley Publishers Ltd®
1 Canada Square
Canary Wharf
London
E14 5AA

For Peter and Keith.

v

"Run!!!" screamed all the little bugs.
"He's coming, we must hide."
And all the mommies of the bugs called out,
"Quick, get inside!"

For climbing up the jagged wall,
with all his gooey might,
Was the ugliest, slimiest, gooiest, slurpiest bug,
Oh what a sight!

"Will anybody play with me?"
Silence – they just stayed still,
They all just held their breaths and waited
watching him until...

He sadly crawled back down the wall
and wriggled to his mom
"I thought I'd heard some bugs above,"
He told her, "now they're gone".

The next day was a wet day
The rain came pouring down
"We're out of juice and porridge,"
Said Ms. Ladybird with a frown.

"Don't worry Mom, I'll get it,
I'll just fly to Bugstore,
I'm bigger now, I know the way,"
And he did love to explore!

So Mom agreed and little ladybird
went out the door,
Feeling very grown up,
Now that he was four!

He flew and jumped and ran and splashed
and played in every puddle.
Then suddenly he tried to move
But couldn't, what a muddle.

"HELP!!!" called tiny ladybird
"I'm stuck! I can't get out!
My legs are stuck, I'm freezing too
Is there anyone about?"

Just then someone came squelching by
and said with a voice so kind,
"Don't worry tiny ladybird
I can grab you from behind".

"Just let me throw this rope to you
Now hold on very tight."
And Uglybug then got to work
and pulled with all his might!

"I'm free! I'm safe! Oh thank you,
You saved me Uglybug!"
"Oh it's no trouble really,
I'm sure that anyone would."

The two bugs then got talking,
Ladybird stood very close,
but didn't mind the drool and snorts
he once had thought were gross!

He saw the fuzz, the slime, the goo
But thought, while standing there,
"This Uglybug's quite cute you know",
perhaps he'd been unfair.

Uglybug went out alone later on that day
and slithered through the forest
exploring all the way.
He loved the sound of nature,
the rustling of the leaves,
the chirping birds, the croaking frogs,
Wind blowing through the trees.

But today he heard a new sound
one he'd never heard before
a gentle little whimper,
he decided to explore.

Down along the babbling brook
beneath the chestnut tree
The sound was getting closer
whatever could it be?

Just then he saw, all curled up small
and shaking with the fear,
a tiny little spider
who did not belong out here.

"I'm lost," sobbed baby spider
"I've been out here all day
I tried to make my way back home
But I couldn't find my way.

My mom will be so worried
She doesn't know I'm here
I'm not supposed to go this far
She says I must stay near."

"Oh you poor, poor baby!
It's going to be okay
don't worry now, I'll take you home
Come on, I'll lead the way."

When they arrived in Bugland,
a search party was on,
and mommy spider shouted,
"Please help! My baby's gone!"

"He's here," said Uglybug quietly,
"I found him safe and sound,
he's just a little shaken,
because no one was around."

17

"You hero!" said mommy spider,
"You wonderful Uglybug,
thank you for saving my baby,"
And she gave him a giant hug!

And as she stood there holding him,
Baby spider by her side,
she couldn't help but notice
his beautiful smile – so wide!

"It's shopping day," said Mommy fly,
"Let's go kids, out the door."
She counted each and every child.
"22, 23, 24!"

They all flew in a perfect line
All the way to Bugstore
Again she counted as they went inside.
"22, 23, 24!"

"Now where's my list?
What do we need?"
She flew up and down each aisle.
With all these hungry mouths to feed,
This was going to take a while.

Also at Bugstore that day
was Uglybug himself,
With pocket money from his mom
he searched on every shelf.

A yoyo or a kite, or perhaps a big ice cream
There was so much he could choose from,
It was every little bug's dream.

Just then he spotted mommy fly,
standing at the till,
"I haven't enough money," she said
staring at the bill.

"Mrs Fly," he said,
"I understand that money must be tight,
Your children can't go hungry,
And I don't need this kite."

He placed the kite back on the shelf,
gave the money to Mrs Fly.
"I'd rather if you have it.
You've important things to buy."

Mrs Fly was speechless,
what a selfless thing to do.
She took his hand and simply said,
"That's really kind, thank you!"

As she stood there holding his little hand,
she noticed something new.
This Uglybug is beautiful,
that face, those eyes so blue.

The ants were super busy,
as ants usually are,
But this day in particular
was the busiest day so far.

For travelling the hills so high
from valleys far away
Was her majesty the queen ant
She was coming here to stay.

"The place must look impeccable,"
said the leader of the ants
"Clean up this mess, pick up those toys,
And water all these plants."

They ran around, so busy,
collecting all the dirt
and determined to impress them all
was a little ant called Bert.

24

He wanted to work hard
He wanted to seem big
So piled up high in his tiny arms
was dirt, sand and a twig.

He kept on piling higher,
hoping everyone could see
I think I'm carrying more than anyone else,
he thought with glee!

Standing watching from afar
was the little Uglybug
watching poor Bert struggle
carrying anything he could.

He watched him sway beneath the weight
of all the twigs and dirt
he could see the pile come tumbling
all around the place, poor Bert!!

"Oh, no!" thought Bert, "Disaster!
I hope no one's watching me".
As he panicked
trying to pick them up
before anyone could see.

Then Uglybug squelched up to him
And whispered, "I'll help you."
"YUCK!" said Bert and moved away
And said, "Eh, no thank you!"

But Uglybug didn't listen
He'd been called much worse than "yuck".
And piled them back into Bert's arms
before anyone could look.

Bert walked away with his highest pile
And the leader said, "Well done!
You can carry such a huge amount
for such a little one."

Bert was feeling very proud
But then he felt quite sad,
If Uglybug had helped him,
then he couldn't be that bad.

He finished up his jobs
And watered all the plants,
"I need to look for Uglybug,"
he called out to the ants.

He found him sitting on a bench
eating by himself
"I'm sorry little Uglybug,
I'm ashamed of myself."

Uglybug looked up at Bert
wiping dribble from his chin.
"Thats quite alright," said Uglybug
Giving Bert a dribbly grin!

"You see everyone is afraid of me
I'm really not sure why
nobody wants to be my friend
no matter how hard I try."

Bert moved a little closer,
And whispered to the bug,
"I'd really like to be your friend,"
and he gave him a giant hug!

Bert looked into his new friend's face
And saw for the first time
His sparkling eyes, the happiest grin,
and fantastic silver slime!

"Will anybody play with me?"
called the little Uglybug.
His new friends all came running
with a high five and a hug!

"Doesn't he look different,"
said ladybird to his mom
"All his scary ugly parts
have vanished they've just gone!

Why does he look so different?
he's not ugly anymore."
"He's been beautiful this whole time,
we've just never looked before,

But now we see whats underneath
what is real and what is true,
his beauty on the inside
is now finally shining through..."

32